MISS ELLA AND
THE TURTLE PEOPLE

Written by Linda B. Schmitz Spangrud

Illustrated by Linda-Bell Schorer

Printed in the United States of America
ISBN 13: 978-1-7339155-0-2

For additional information or to schedule a book signing
and reading, please visit www.Spangrud.com or email Linda
B. Schmitz Spangrud at LindaBSpangrud@gmail.com.

Dedicated to my family. Husband Tom, Son Adam,
Daughter-in-law, Brittany and Grandson Jack.
They are always there for me.

With Love ♥,
Linda B. Spangud

Turtle People are people who volunteer to help protect sea turtles. They come from all over the world. Turtle people are young and old. They are big and little.

Turtle People have many different jobs. Some are teachers, nurses, doctors, firemen, policemen, bakers, artists, builders, and computer technicians.

Turtle People are all unique. They are passionate about turtles.

Turtle People have one thing in common, their love for turtles and the ocean where turtles live. Turtle People are just that, Turtle People.

This story is about Miss Ella and the Turtle People. When Miss Ella was a little girl, she went to the beach every summer with her parents.

She grew up and got married. Miss Ella and her husband took their children to the beach every summer.

Miss Ella and her husband loved the beach so much they decided to build a house there.

They were so happy in their beach house for a very long time.

Then, one day Miss Ella's husband became sick and died, leaving Miss Ella in the beach house all alone. She was very sad, until one day...

17

Miss Ella saw a group of people on the beach. She wondered what they were doing. She went and asked them. They were measuring tracks where a mama sea turtle crawled onto the beach the night before. This is the day Miss Ella met the Turtle People.

Miss Ella learned that mama sea turtles lay their eggs deep in the sand late at night. She learned that sea turtles can lay over 100 eggs in a nest.

Miss Ella learned that sometimes Turtle People must dig up turtle nests. They carefully move the eggs farther away from the water to keep them safe from big waves.

Miss Ella learned that sea turtles, such as Loggerheads and Kemp's Ridley, are on the endangered species list. Turtle People became involved to help save these sea turtles. Miss Ella was learning a lot from her new friends, the Turtle People.

She learned that bright lights from condos and hotels can lead baby turtles in the wrong direction when they hatch. The lights can lead the baby turtles towards the dangerous street away from their safe home in the ocean.

Miss Ella learned that Turtle People sometimes stay up all night to babysit the turtle nests. They protect the baby turtles from other animals like foxes, crabs, and birds that try to eat them. They want to make sure the baby turtles go to the ocean when they hatch and not to the street.

In all her years at the beach, Miss Ella had never seen baby turtles hatch. She wanted to see that very much. She would dream about seeing the baby turtles charge to the ocean. She thought about it all day long.

Then one night a mother sea turtle laid a nest in front of Miss Ella's house. She was so happy. She watched the nest day and night. Miss Ella begged the Turtle People to please wake her up if she was sleeping when the turtles hatch. She promised she would rush out anytime of the day or night to help.

Miss Ella learned that Turtle People start babysitting the nest at night 55 days after the eggs are laid. They babysit the nest through all kinds of weather. While the Turtle People were babysitting the nest, Miss Ella offered them water when they were thirsty, snacks when they were hungry, a blanket when it was cool, and an umbrella when it rained. The Turtle People became very good friends with Miss Ella.

Miss Ella saw the Turtle People use a stethoscope to listen to the nest, the same way a doctor listens to your heart. The noise the Turtle People hear in the sand tells them how soon the baby turtles will hatch and crawl out. They babysat one night. Then two nights. Then three nights. Then four nights. They became best friends with Miss Ella. On the fifth night at 10:00 P.M., the first baby turtle poked his head out of the sand. He is called the scout.

Everyone became so excited. The Turtle People rushed quickly to get Miss Ella. She was in bed and came out in her pajamas. The Turtle People guided Miss Ella to the nest.

Miss Ella made it to the nest just as all the baby turtles started crawling out. This is called a boil. All the baby turtles come rushing out of the nest at the same time. The sand boils over like a pot of boiling water. The baby turtles then start their march to the sea.

39

There was excitement everywhere. The moon was bright. The baby turtles started crawling down the trench dug by the Turtle People. This trench leads them to the welcoming waves and open ocean. This trench helps the baby turtles go towards the safe water and not the busy street.

Everyone was so excited to see 112 baby turtles start their life by marching to the sea.

The Turtle People named the first little turtle Miss Ella in honor of Miss Ella. Miss Ella smiled so brightly and giggled just like the little girl she used to be all those years ago.

Miss Ella loves sea turtles just like the Turtle People. Miss Ella has many new friends and is not alone any more. She is now a Turtle Person and dreams of baby turtles.

Turtle People come from all over the world. They come in all ages and all sizes. Turtle People are passionate and unique. Turtle People are volunteers that have one thing in common, the love for the turtles and the oceans where the turtles live. Turtle People are just that, Turtle People

New Vocabulary for Little Listeners

Volunteer
Protect
Passionate
Unique
Common
Safe
Endangered
Species
Loggerheads
Kemp's Ridleys
Hatch
Nest
Stethoscope
Guided
Boil
Trench
Volunteers

Author

Linda B. Schmitz Spangrud grew up in Iowa and spent her career as a teacher, principal, and school district administrator in Illinois. Family and people are very important to her. She loves children's books and read many books to her students, son and grandson. She is passionate about reading and learning. Her zest for living includes writing, reading, golfing, music and travel. She is an active volunteer in her community. When moving to the Alabama Gulf Coast with her husband Tom in 2006, they became involved in the sea turtle (Share the Beach) program. They have been volunteers ever since.

Illustrator

Linda-Bell Schorer, originally from Canada, is a free lance artist who makes her home in Gulf Shores, Alabama. She is passionate about design, illustration, and pottery. Linda draws her inspiration from nature. She loves spending times with her cats. Linda enjoys coastal living and dedicates her spare time as a volunteer with the Share the Beach, Alabama's sea turtle program.

CPSIA information can be obtained
at www.ICGtesting.com
Printed in the USA
BVHW020246251019
562049BV00001B/1/P